It's Halloween,

Jane Smith

Albert Whitman & Company
Chicago, Illinois

It's Halloween!

Halloween is an autumn tradition.

Every year my family carves pumpkins into spooky jack-o'-lanterns. My mommy makes homemade cinnamon-sugar doughnuts and apple cider.

My daddy hangs glow-in-the-dark skeletons
and fake spiders in our yard.

Tonight all the kids in my neighborhood will dress up in costumes. Then they'll walk door-to-door saying, "trick or treat," and all the neighbors will fill their treat bags with candy and goodies! Yum!

Mary Margaret, George, and I are going trick-or-treating together. Before they come over, I put on my Princess Kitty costume. Blue dress, check! Crown, check! Kitty ears, check!

My mommy even brushes real makeup on my cheeks.
My Halloween costume is perfect!

Then I wait outside for my friends to arrive.

The night is dark and the jack-o'-lanterns are glowing.
It's a little spooky!

I'm happy when Mary Margaret, George, and their families walk up the front steps. "Happy Halloween!" calls out Mary Margaret.

"Boo!" says George. He's dressed up as a ghost!

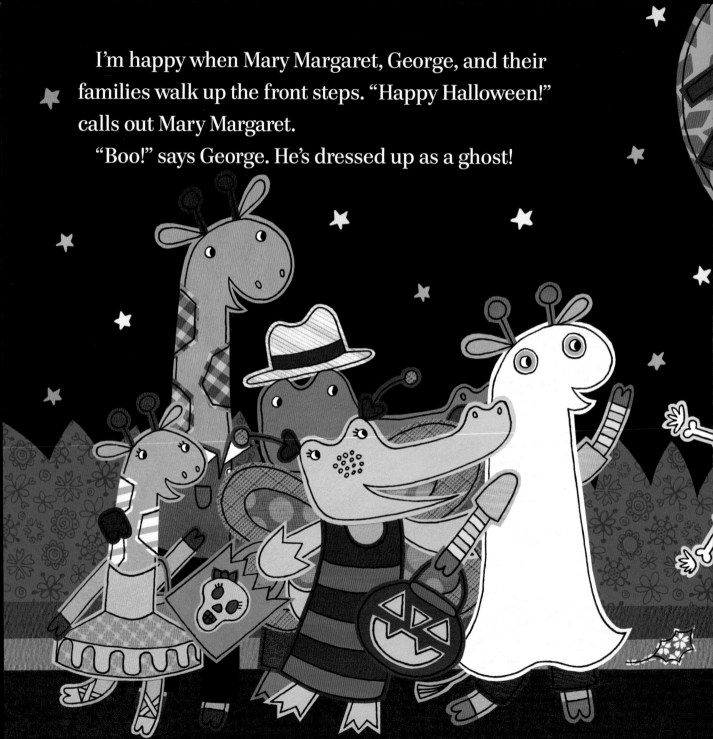

We agree to go to every house on our block so we can
get as much candy as possible.

"But I think we should skip the old, creepy house on the corner," I say. "Leo told me that an evil witch lives there."

"There's no such thing as an evil witch," says Mary Margaret. "Don't worry, Chloe Zoe!"

"Let's go get some candy!"
George grins.
   "Yes!" I smile, and we are
ready to start trick-or-treating.

We all walk up to the first house together. George rings the doorbell—ding-dong!—and everyone hollers, "Trick or treat!"

A nice lady dressed as a black cat comes to the door and drops little packages of candy corn into each of our treat bags. Yay!

Up and down the street,
we trick-or-treat, stopping
at every house along the
way. Our treat bags fill
up with lots and lots of
chocolates, lollipops,
and candies all wrapped
in orange, purple,
and green foil.

We see lots of fun costumes too—a robot,
a ladybug, and a superhero!

But soon there's only one house left: the old, creepy one.
I freeze at the gate as Mary Margaret hurries up the path.

"Mary Margaret," I whisper, "what about the witch?"

"I'm sure even witches give out candy on Halloween!"
says George.

"Chloe Zoe, remember—there's no such thing as an
evil witch," says Mary Margaret.

But I still feel scared. My heart is thumping
superfast. Mary Margaret and George run ahead
to ring the doorbell. The house is shadowy
and it creaks and squeaks. And then I see
a witch on the porch!

I scream and run back
to my daddy.

"That house is TOO scary!" I cry.
"I don't want the witch to get us!"

My daddy hugs me tight. "There's
no such thing as a witch. You and
your friends are safe."

Mary Margaret and George come running over. "Don't be scared, Chloe Zoe!" says Mary Margaret.

"We met Mrs. Elena and she has an extra-special Halloween treat for us!" adds George.

I look up at my daddy, and he smiles. "Go on if you want to," he says. "There's nothing to be afraid of."

Mary Margaret takes one of my hands and George takes the other. I feel a lot braver all of a sudden. Together we walk up to the old house.

When I get to the porch, I see that the witch is actually Mrs. Elena dressed up like a scarecrow. Not scary at all!

"Happy Halloween!" says Mrs. Elena. "What a cute Princess Kitty, butterfly, and ghost!" Then she drops a *giant* candy bar into each of our treat bags.

"Thank you!" I smile.

When we get home, Mary Margaret, George, and I sort through all our candy. Mrs. Elena's giant candy bars are the best treat of all!

"This is the yummiest Halloween ever!" cheers George.

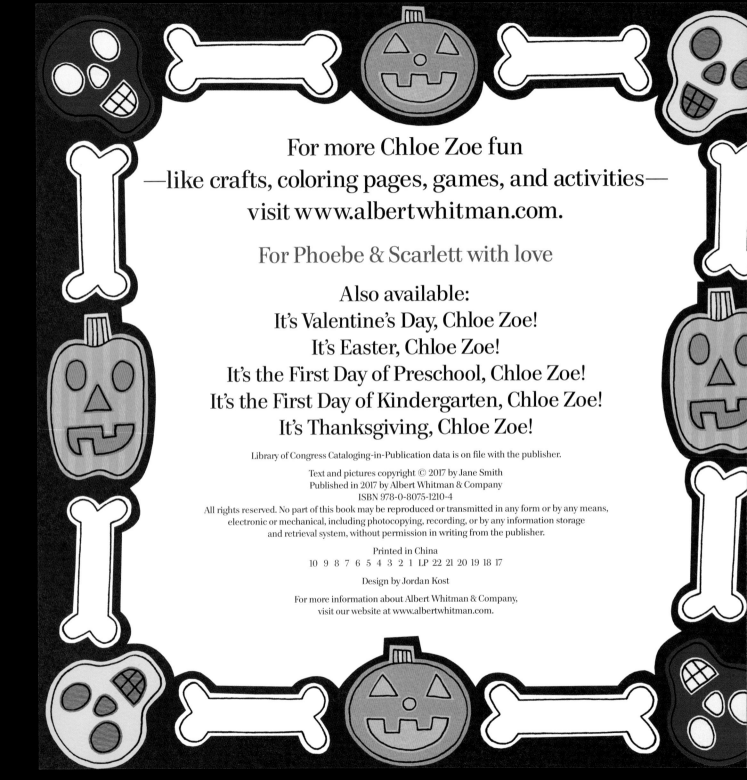

For more Chloe Zoe fun
—like crafts, coloring pages, games, and activities—
visit www.albertwhitman.com.

For Phoebe & Scarlett with love

Also available:
It's Valentine's Day, Chloe Zoe!
It's Easter, Chloe Zoe!
It's the First Day of Preschool, Chloe Zoe!
It's the First Day of Kindergarten, Chloe Zoe!
It's Thanksgiving, Chloe Zoe!

Library of Congress Cataloging-in-Publication data is on file with the publisher.

Text and pictures copyright © 2017 by Jane Smith
Published in 2017 by Albert Whitman & Company
ISBN 978-0-8075-1210-4
Printed in China
10 9 8 7 6 5 4 3 2 1 LP 22 21 20 19 18 17

Design by Jordan Kost

For more information about Albert Whitman & Company,
visit our website at www.albertwhitman.com.